Curious George

AT THE BALLET

Adapted from the Curious George film series
edited by Margret Rey and Alan J. Shalleck

1 9 8 6

Houghton Mifflin Company Boston

Library of Congress Cataloging-in-Publication Data

Curious George at the ballet.

"Adapted from the Curious George film series."
Summary: George goes to the ballet but his curiosity
interferes with the performance.
[1. Monkeys—Fiction. 2. Ballet dancing—Fiction]
I. Rey, Margret. II. Shalleck, Alan J. III. Curious
George at the ballet (Motion picture) IV. Title.
PZ7.C92127 1986 [E] 86-7469
ISBN 0-395-42477-1 RNF
ISBN 0-395-42474-7 PAP

Copyright © 1986 by Houghton Mifflin Company and Curgeo Agencies, Inc.

Printed in Japan

DNP 10 9 8 7 6 5 4 3 2 1

George was excited. The man with the yellow hat
was taking him to the theater
to see their friend Pedro dance.

Inside the theater, all the dancers
were getting ready for the show.

And there was their friend Pedro.
He was wearing short pants
and a shirt with patches all over it.

"We are dancing the story
of Jack and the Beanstalk tonight,
and I'm playing Jack," Pedro said.

"First I will plant these magic beans
and then, when the beanstalk grows,
I'll climb up to the sky."

Suddenly the beanstalk began to rise.

It rose right to the top of the theater!

How did that happen? George was curious.

Then he saw a man in a black jacket
at the top of the stage.

"After Pedro plants the magic beans," the man said,
"I pull this wire and the people in the audience
think the beanstalk is really growing."

"Now it's time for you to take your seat, George,"
he said. "The show is about to begin."

On the way to his seat,
George saw a big, painted mask.
He was curious.

He put it over his head.
It was so big that it covered him
right to his toes.

It was dark inside the mask.
George couldn't see where he was going,
but he heard people laughing.

George had walked onstage
just as Pedro began to dance!

The people in the audience
were laughing so hard that Pedro had to stop.

"George," he whispered angrily,
"get off the stage. I'm in the middle of my dance!"

George was scared. He pushed off the mask
and ran up the ladder to the top of the stage.

Pedro had started to dance again
and was planting the magic beans.

George watched from the top of the stage.

Then he noticed the man in the black jacket.
The man was in trouble.
The wire from the magic beanstalk had broken!

But George knew what to do.
He put on the man's black jacket so no one would see him,
and leaped to the back of the stage.

How good that George was a monkey!

Quickly, he climbed down the curtain
and grabbed the wire.

George climbed up and handed the wire
back to the man.

The beanstalk grew.
Now Pedro could climb right to the top.

The audience cheered.
"Bravo! Bravo!"

After the curtain came down,
Pedro turned to George.
"You saved the show," he said.

When the curtain went up again,
George took a bow with Pedro.
"Hooray for Pedro!" the audience shouted.

"And hooray for George!"
The man with the yellow hat
clapped the loudest of all.